The Mystery Troublemakers

Peter Marney

ISBN-13: 978-1975667757

ISBN-10: 1975667751

This book is dedicated to those who share their smiles with the world.

Read this first

You are not a ninja.

 It's very important that you keep
remembering this.

 If you try to copy any of the
stuff in this book then you might
end up in prison.

 Even if you copy just some of this
stuff, you'll end up in trouble.

This will be bad.

This will be very bad because I'll get the blame.

So please, remember you're not a ninja and promise not to try and copy me.

Have you promised?

Ok, you can now read on.

My first fight

It's funny how things go round in circles.

There I was a few months ago about to get into my first ever real fight and here I am again, facing one of the same Monster Twins, and about to get hit.

Last time I got saved by Big Jay but now all he's doing is standing and watching.

No, that's not true.

He's also shouting at me.

"Come on, get stuck in!"

Helpful.

Before I get killed I think I should say hello.

I'm Jamie. I'm nearly ten years old and I'm about to get thumped.

As usual, it's Keira's fault.

She's my sort of babysitter, judo teacher, and I suppose the leader of our secret ninja clan. I'll tell you a bit more about that later but someone's just rung a bell and Monster Boy is on his way over to try and hit me.

He'll probably succeed.

He's a bit bigger than me, and has been in more fights than me, so I guess he knows what he's doing. All

I've learned is what Red taught me before we got here tonight.

She's a girl but don't let that fool you. She's the best fighter on the estate these days and luckily my best friend as well.

I'm sort of hiding behind my fists and moving about a bit to try and stay out of range. All this does is allow Monster Boy to keep coming forward.

He's jabbing with his right hand but my arms are blocking the punches and it doesn't hurt too much. Then he swings with his left trying to knock my head off.

I duck under the punch and jab a fist into his unprotected belly. That slows him up a bit and we both start dancing around each other.

Not real dancing. That would be silly and anyway there's no music and I dance like a muppet according to Red. We just sort of circle each other while Big Jay keeps shouting, "Stop messing about and hit him!"

I'm not sure which one of us he's shouting at but decide that, as he's Red's scary cousin, he should be on my side.

Monster Boy drops his right hand ready to jab me in the ribs but I get a thump into the side of his head first and he falls over.

Then that bell rings again and we both stop fighting.

"Not bad for a first time Jamie," says Big Jay. "Up you get Oli."

Oli?

The Monster Boy's got a name?

I know he goes to my school but we don't see much of Year Six and I've tried to keep out of the way of the Twins following our last meeting.

So that was my first and only real fight and I think I won.

I'm not sure because I don't know the rules but I guess that knocking over your opponent sort of counts for something.

As I said, this is all Keira's fault.

She decided that school judo wasn't really helping me much even though I was getting a bit better at it and didn't always end up looking at the ceiling.

So we're here.

Here is the local youth club which technically I'm too young to join but being nearly ten sort of counts as okay.

It turns out that Big Jay is one of the leaders and tonight is boxing night. Twice a week he teaches people how to box and then once a year they have a competition.

No, I haven't won the competition as this is only a training bout and not even in a proper ring, although we are wearing boxing gloves and head guards. I don't think new members are usually allowed to do this but Keira got Jay to let me try.

She's good at getting me into trouble is Keira.

Red shouldn't be here either but the rules don't seem to apply to her maybe because she's in Year Five. I guess being Jay's cousin also helps, plus the fact that nobody in their right mind is going to want to upset Red.

When she gets really angry she sort of forgets any rules and fights to win. I've seen her fight like that a couple of times and it's not nice.

Jay brings Oli over and we have to shake hands.

"Not bad for a first time," says Oli, "but you got lucky with that last punch."

Jay shakes his head.

"No he didn't Oli, you let him in and he was quick enough to hit you first. You should thank him for showing you a weak spot. Don't go for the body as a first shot. It leaves your head open for attack."

Oli seems to know what all this means and nods.

Then he smiles at me and says, "Well done Jamie and thanks."

Nobody's ever thanked me for hitting them before but I suppose I've never really hit anyone properly. Maybe this is what you're supposed to do after a fight.

"Yeah, er thanks Oli," I say, still a bit confused.

This isn't how I expected the night to go.

Peter Marney

More training

On the way home Keira seems happy.

"Looks like a good gym Jamie," she says, "and Jay knows what he's talking about."

How Keira knows what's good and what's not is a mystery to me but most things about Keira are

9

blurred. Like me, she's very good at not talking about herself.

She turned up one night as an emergency baby-sitter so that Mum could go out with the girls and she's been doing the same thing twice a week ever since. I guess Mum trusts her.

I usually like Keira but sometimes she gets us into more trouble than I'm happy with.

Us, by the way, are the Red Sock Ninja Clan. It's a big secret and only four of us know it exists. Me, Red, Keira, and Wally who is at home tonight with his baby sister.

Sometimes I wish I had a baby sister to use as an excuse to keep me out of trouble.

As well as apparently knowing about gyms and boxing, Keira is also good at judo and Kung Fu.

She secretly teaches us all sorts of stuff which isn't exactly legal, like how to follow people and how to pick locks. This is a way of unlocking a door or window or padlock without using the key.

It even works with handcuffs but that's another story.

Keira gave me some lock picks for Christmas and now I'm nearly as good as Red at getting through a locked door.

Red comes from this really big family who most people think are a bunch of criminals. This isn't true. Well, not totally true and Red doesn't get into trouble at all unless it's with the rest of us.

We've never officially been in proper trouble but have had to do some naughty things in the past so that some bad guys got caught instead of getting away with stuff. As a Clan we're also good at running away from policemen and hiding, which is the main reason why we've never been in trouble.

Every secret ninja is supposed to have a special skill.

As I've said, Red is a fighter and good at getting into locked places.

Wally, because he's so tall, is a really good climber and is also good at coming up with cunning plans. He doesn't think too fast but when he does start thinking it's usually worth waiting for.

Me?

I'm not good at anything much except maybe following people. Apparently I'm the sort of boy who can get lost in a crowd and disappear. The sort of face that's instantly forgettable. I think this is a good thing but it's hardly a special skill.

Instead of taking the main road home, Keira has turned off onto a side street.

"Time for some training, ninja boy," she says.

Now what trouble is she going to get me into?

It's actually worse than that.

She starts jogging.

"Come on Jamie, you need to build up some fitness if you're going to be a boxer."

I didn't know I was going to be a boxer and I hate running. But it's keep up with Keira or be lost on some side street in the dark.

Anyway, she's got my front door key and I've come out without my lock picks so I need that key to get to bed tonight.

Five minutes later and just when I'm running out of breath, Keira stops to go shopping.

Typical girl.

It's one of those corner shops which never seems to close and has a bell which rings as you go in.

"Hello Mr Patel, how are you today sir?" she says to the man behind the counter.

Does Keira know everyone?

The man nods to her.

"Miss Keira, why is there nobody in this town with your good manners? Why is there so little respect?"

He doesn't look happy.

"But no, I should not share my troubles. Who is this young man you have brought to see me?"

Keira puts her arm around my shoulder.

"He's a friend Mr Patel. Say hello Jamie."

Behind my back, Keira is tapping my shoulder. I think she is trying to tell me something so I decide to be super polite.

"Hello Mr Patel, I'm pleased to meet you."

I hold out my hand and he shakes it, smiling at me.

"And I'm pleased to meet you too Jamie."

Keira asks about his family and buys a bottle of water. She tells him that we're out on a run and asks him for the time so she can check our speed.

There's a clock on the wall so why she didn't just look there I'm not sure. Anyway, she didn't say she was timing me and I don't need timing. I already know I'm slow.

We say goodbye and then after a small glug of water, we're back running home again.

By the time we get there I'm worn out. I have a quick shower and then get to bed, leaving Keira watching the telly until Mum comes home.

I'm so tired I go straight to sleep and don't even have to count sheep in my head which is what I usually do when I can't sleep.

I've been doing that a lot lately but not tonight.

Tonight I will dream about being a secret fighting ninja.

Peter Marney

Fight night

Why do people make such a fuss about birthdays?

Yesterday I was nine years old and today I'm ten.

So what?

I'm just another day older than I was yesterday and there's no need to make a fuss.

In the Olden Days, nobody really knew what day they were born on so I guess nobody had a birthday or a party or any of the other silly stuff that goes on these days.

I'm not having a party. I didn't want one and Mum isn't bothered so it isn't happening.

I also asked Miss not to make a fuss at school and she agreed. She did whisper "Happy Birthday" to me when nobody else was near but that was all.

I like Miss S.

Gran sent a card and some money which I put in my piggy bank and Mum gave me a card as well. They're both now hidden under my bed.

Keira said "Happy Birthday" that evening so I guess Mum must have told her. Mum's rubbish at keeping my secrets.

We're off to the youth club again tonight and more boxing but hopefully no more jogging.

All is not well when we get there.

Apparently some of the kids have been causing trouble in the local area and Big Jay isn't happy.

"We've got this building 'cos the owner wants to help out local kids. Why's he going to keep doing that if you lot are causing trouble?"

He's not happy at all.

Everybody says it wasn't them which is sensible. If I'd got into trouble, I wouldn't tell Big Jay while he's still angry.

But listening to people later in the evening it seems that nobody knows anything about any trouble at all. Nobody even looks like they know something either.

I'm getting good at watching people and can usually tell when something is going on or someone's lying.

Like in school when the toilet sort of fell off the wall. I could tell in the playground who was involved just by looking at who was talking to who and who was behaving a bit suspicious.

Nobody is looking suspicious now, not even Oli the Monster Twin.

Me, Red and Keira stay behind afterwards to put things away. This is being helpful but I think it's just so Keira can ask questions.

The club is above a coffee shop which we can also use on club nights. The rest of the block are shops as well, although most look sort of run down a bit.

Seems the owners are complaining that the club kids are being a problem and generally misbehaving although nobody can say what the troublemakers look like.

I'm thinking about this and so miss what happens next but suddenly Keira and Jay are arguing.

"No."

"Why not?"

"No, just no!"

"Afraid I'll beat you?"

I think Keira is challenging Jay to a fight. It sounds like the sort of thing Keira would do.

Red seems to like the idea.

"Come on Jay, fight her!"

I find out later that Jay doesn't want girls fighting in his gym and Keira didn't like that idea so she challenged him. At the moment I don't know any of this so I'm very confused.

Jay clearly doesn't want to fight but, with Keira and Red both happy with the idea, he doesn't stand a chance.

"You box or whatever and I'll freestyle," says Keira.

"The ring is these mats and if it makes you happier, we'll both wear helmets."

Jay puts his boxing gloves on and Keira slips off her trainers and socks.

"Boxing rules?" he asks as they both put on their helmets.

"Not likely," says Keira and aims a kick at his head.

He ducks back and they both start dancing around each other.

No, there's still no music.

Jay closes in and jabs at Keira's head guard but she sort of rolls to the side clipping his leg as she goes past and bringing him to the ground.

Before he can move, she's on her feet again and has kicked him in the knee before backing away.

Jay now looks angry and is hurrying forward to punch Keira as quickly as he can.

But first he has to catch her. She keeps ducking around him, each time hitting him on the arm as she slides by.

Then she runs to the corner of the mats, puts her hands up in surrender and bows just like we do in judo.

"Had enough?" Jay asks.

Keira smiles.

"No. But you can't fight with two broken arms and a busted knee."

I'm confused because Jay doesn't look hurt at all.

"You're dreaming girl," he says. "You've hardly touched me."

Keira has moved over to the big punching bag.

I've already used this bag and it's really hard and heavy. None of us kids can shift it much no matter how hard we punch.

"I pulled my punches. Felt sorry for you and didn't use full power. If I'd really tried, this would have happened."

She aims two punches at the bag, swings round and then kicks it.

We all watch the bag swinging backwards and forwards with the power of her hits.

"Now tell me that girls can't fight," she says.

Jay isn't convinced.

He puts his gloves in front of his chest.

"Come on then, free shot. Let's see you hit my gloves with all you've got."

Is he mad? Hasn't he seen what she's just done to that innocent bag?

The next bit happens rather fast but ends up with Jay flying backwards and landing on his bum.

I think he's convinced now.

Keira's putting her trainers back on so I guess the fight is over.

"Let's have a chat next week about letting girls fight. I've got to get Jamie home now. Come on Jamie, time to go. Bye."

The Mystery Troublemakers

Looks like it's time to leave.

When I get outside, Keira starts to jog home so I don't get the chance to ask questions until we get to Mr Patel's shop.

"How did you do that?" I ask.

"Years of training Jamie and from someone who's not scared to let girls fight."

Then we're in the shop and asking about Mr Patel's week and family and the usual polite stuff we're supposed to do when we meet people.

The jog home is still hard work but I'm sleeping a lot better these days. My sheep might have to find someone else to count them.

Peter Marney

Hats

Miss has decided that we need some fresh air so we're all on the field in our shorts.

I really enjoy PE.

Not!

What's the point in running round in big circles? Or throwing things just so you can go and pick them up again?

To warm up, Miss sends us running around the edge of the school field. I notice that she doesn't join in.

I also notice that I'm not in my usual place at the back with Andrew. He's slow and fat but we're not supposed to mention it in case he gets upset.

Keira's jogging sessions must be making a difference because I'm now keeping up with the sporty kids.

These are the ones who's Mums and Dads take them to swimming and tennis and football and netball and whatever else they happen to be good at. I guess they want to have them running around somewhere else rather than spending time at home.

Anyway, Miss has just shouted at us to do another lap and I'm starting to catch up with the leaders.

Usually they're catching up with me. Well, they're usually finishing their second lap as I'm finishing my first.

But today is different.

Today I finish the race in the top ten which I've never done in any race in my life before, except for the sack race in the infants when there were only ten of us in the class.

I still came last though.

As usual Miss is saying "Well done" to everyone for a good effort no matter where they came in the race.

She jogs into the middle of the field and gets all of us to follow.

We're not supposed to notice but this means that the slower ones don't have to finish their second lap or, in Andrew's case, his first lap.

We then play some other games where we have to work together rather than against each other. I like these sort of games as we all get a chance to join in. Even Miss sort of joins in but she still keeps her coat and silly hat on.

Have I mentioned that Miss has a collection of silly hats?

Some of these are for the classroom when she's pretending to be someone else and some are for the playground when she looks after us.

I'm not sure what Mrs Wallace, our head teacher, thinks of these hats but she did smile when she caught Miss wearing the rabbit ears during a lesson. Miss was being the "Giant Bunny of Punctuation" to remind us to put a full stop at the end of our sentences and a capital letter at the beginning.

Yes, I know it sounds silly but it helps remind us what we need to be doing.

Actually I just sort of guess when it comes to sentences and full stops as I'm not sure when they're supposed to end so these lessons aren't my favourite but the rabbit ears help.

I wonder why every teacher doesn't use them?

Peter Marney

Suspicion

Something odd is happening.

Big Jay has had the owner of the building on to him again. People are still complaining about the youth club kids causing trouble even though none of us know anything about it.

This time there's proof.

One of the shop owners says he spotted one of the boys wearing a

hoodie with the name of our club on
the back so it's got to be our
fault.

This is odd because our club
doesn't allow hoodies. It's one of
Jay's things.

"Everyone's scared of you guys
'cause you look like trouble
wearing hoodies and joggers. So, no
more hoodies. You wearing a hoodie,
you ain't coming in. Got it?"

Red says that Jay works as a
bouncer sometimes.

I thought this must have something
to do with trampolines but she says
it means he stands outside clubs or
pubs and stops the wrong sort of
people going in. So why is he
called a bouncer and not a stander?

Anyway, this so called proof is
very strange because we don't have
our club name on the back of
anything because we can't afford
it.

So who is going around wearing a club hoodie when we don't have club hoodies?

Keira thinks this is a job for the Red Sock Ninjas and I agree.

That's why I'm standing at this bus stop pretending to wait for a bus I don't need. I'm not going into the club so I've got my hoodie pulled up and some earphones plugged in with the wire tucked in my pocket. Shame there's nothing to plug them into.

It's a disguise.

Like this I just blend into the background.

Red and Keira are lurking somewhere at the end of the street ready to tail anyone suspicious while Wally is doing the same thing at the other end of the block. Anyone causing trouble tonight will be in for a surprise.

Instead it's me who gets the surprise.

A man comes out of one of the closed shops trying to look innocent.

He looks like someone who doesn't want to be seen doing something he shouldn't be doing. Perhaps he's just knocked a toilet off a wall.

He hurries off and then another pair of men come out of the same shop doing the same thing.

That's a lot of toilets.

The next man coming out just walks down to the next door shop and unlocks it before going in. I think he must own it.

In all I count seven men coming out of the one shop and heading off in different directions, except for the three who go into what I assume are their own shops. This is beginning to look like a secret meeting.

So why are the local shopkeepers meeting in secret and who are the other men?

I'd like to follow one of them but I'm supposed to be here to catch our troublemakers so I stay where I am and wait for our hoodie wearers to show up.

An hour later and Keira passes with Red on the way to give Wally the secret signal to go home. I decide to forget the bus and walk, maybe take a short cut down one of the side streets.

Really I'm going to wait outside Mr Patel's for the rest of the clan so we can go home together. Maybe we'll jog and I'll see if I can keep up with Wally and his long legs.

But before then, Keira takes us all inside the shop so she can chat to Mr Patel and so that he can meet Red and Wally.

As usual we get to hear all about his family and we also meet one of his sons who has a funny name which I don't hear properly.

I must have a problem with foreign names because I can never say Miss S's proper name either.

That's because she's half Polish and has a name with letters which aren't supposed to go together and don't sound out anything except something that could be a sneeze.

Mr Patel isn't Polish though. He tells me that his family came from India and shows me where it is on a map. It's about halfway to Australia so it must be a long way away because Australia is on the other side of the world.

He's pleased to meet my friends and they shake hands with him and his son.

Keira must have told them what to do on the way here as I've never seen either of them shake hands before. Red has shaken her fist at me a few times but that's different and anyway she was sort of joking, I hope.

On the jog home I tell the others about the strange men. Yes, I can now jog and talk at the same time and I'm even managing to keep up with Wally.

Maybe the meeting wasn't anything unusual but Keira thinks we should mention it to Jay just in case.

I'm sure something suspicious is going on.

Nobody tries to look that innocent if they haven't just knocked something off of a wall.

Peter Marney

Hide and seek

Judo night has been turned upside down.

Instead of me looking up at the school ceiling I'm now looking down at the floor and my opponent who I've just thrown.

He tried to "O Goshi" me but instead I just lifted him up and dumped him on the floor. Not really a proper judo throw but the end result was good from my point of view although we both look a bit surprised.

Sensei Keira has noticed as well.

"Jamie, stop freestyling," she says. "Use the throws I've taught you."

Didn't notice her using proper throws when she beat Big Jay.

We start fighting again and I manage to trick him into a "Dashy Harry" which ends up with me dropping him onto the floor again.

"Jamie, swap with Wally please."

I bow to my opponent like Sensei Keira insists we do and then swap.

Thanks Keira.

Now I'm fighting Monster Oli who's just joined the judo club. This time we don't have boxing gloves or head guards.

We bow to each other before we start and Oli grins at me.

"Best of three rounds?" he asks.

He puts his hands up like he's going to box me before dropping them and coming forward properly.

Oli is in Year Six and is bigger and stronger than me. This isn't always an advantage in judo but he still manages to tip me onto my bottom after a couple of minutes.

Hello ceiling.

Round One to Oli.

When I'm back on my feet he tries for a quick throw before I can get a grip on him but I skip out of the way and push him off balance. He'd normally just stagger a bit but I've nudged his leg enough so that it collapses under him and it's his bottom's turn to hit the floor.

My round I think and we're level with one throw each.

We're both now freestyling and looking for an opening or weakness in the other's defence.

When I fight these days I sort of stop looking. It's hard to describe but I'm sort of looking everywhere and nowhere. Red says I should be looking at my opponent's eyes but this is difficult for me to do so, instead, I fight my way.

Neither of us are getting anywhere. We both try jiggling this way and that in an attempt to get the other off balance but it just isn't working.

I'm getting bored and it's nearly time to go home so I relax my guard and let Oli make an easy throw. I know this isn't what we're supposed to be doing but there again, we're not supposed to be freestyling at all.

Oli looks puzzled.

"Did you just let me do that?" he asks.

I grin. He can work it out for himself later.

Keira shouts for us all to stop and we end the session by bowing to her as we're supposed to do for some reason.

She keeps the Red Socks back to help tidy up and then shows us all a key.

"Guess who gets to lock up tonight?" she asks.

Now even the caretaker is trusting her and has gone home early.

We're told to stay in the hall until she's turned off all the lights in the school. Then we play ninja hide and seek for a while.

I'm getting better at this game and have worked out to use my ears more than my eyes. I walk about silently with my mouth half open listening for any little noise which will tell me where anyone is hiding.

It's a bit like when I was fighting Oli but different. I'm sort of here but trying to be everywhere.

I've already worked out that Wally is on top of the cupboard in the other Year Four classroom but I'm not sure how he managed to get up there. He really does climb like one of those lizards with sticky feet.

I decide to leave Wally where he is and go searching up in Year Six.

I'm standing very still in the corridor with my eyes closed and my mouth open. Someone is here. I can sense it.

Slowly I creep forward, turning my head from side to side trying to pick up the smallest sound. Somehow I just know that it's Keira even if I can't see her yet.

She's in here somewhere.

I make my way around the first classroom not looking anywhere special. I'm just trying to sense any small changes in anything.

There it is.

Just to be sure, I pretend to double back a bit but then return to where I was, paying attention to the deep shadows right in the corner of the room.

Now that I'm certain, I turn around and head towards the door.

"Bye Keira."

Time to find Red who I think has been following me and so is now probably hiding in a classroom I've already searched.

She can be sneaky sometimes can Red.

Peter Marney

Rubbish

I seem to be going backwards with my reading.

Did I mention that I read like a six year old?

Miss says I have a sort of disease although it's not a proper disease. It just stops my brain from seeing words properly.

I should be able to read by now but I'm having to spend all of my time decoding words. Even with my good memory, this is a problem but Miss doesn't seem to mind.

"I'm really rubbish at this aren't I Miss?"

Let's see if she tells the truth.

"Yes Jamie, total rubbish."

It sounds rude but she's grinning.

"I mean, you're hardly trying. You've just spent the last five minutes staring out of the window counting flying pigs."

I think Miss is joking.

Actually I've spent those five minutes struggling through two pages of my reading book with Miss helping every so often.

"Of course you're not rubbish Jamie. You're trying as hard as you can and I can't expect more than that from anyone in my class."

I still can't read properly though can I?

"We can't all be good at everything Jamie. Take me, I'm

totally rubbish at PE and I still can't ride a bike."

I didn't know that.

"I can tell you something else you're better at than me Jamie."

This sounds unlikely.

"I'm totally rubbish at being Jamie, whereas you're the world's expert. There's nobody else in the whole world who's better at being Jamie than you."

I'd never thought of it like that before.

"I love this class but if I could have a few more Jamies I'd be just as happy."

Really?

I'm not sure I'd like to have a few more of me running around in school. I'd get confused.

I wonder if Red would be able to spot the real me?

I close my book and go back to my desk to think about a world filled with lots of copies of me.

I suppose it might be a bit like being a Pike.

Red's got lots of family and I guess that some of them must be a bit like her though none of them have red hair or use their teeth when fighting as far as I know.

Finding myself in the school photo would be difficult as well if there were lots of me.

In the main corridor there's a whole line of school photos going back until when Year Six were in Reception. I can't pick out Oli but in another photo I can see Wally in Year One and Red in Year Two.

I'm only in the latest photo and Miss S is only in two of them as she's fairly new to the school as well. Mrs Wallace is in all of them like some of the other teachers.

They all look a bit younger in the early photos though and some are wearing odd looking clothes. Mr Brown also has hair in the first photo which looks really strange.

It's like a time machine in a frame.

Actually the Red Sock Ninjas could use a time machine right now.

We've spent three evenings watching the shops surrounding the youth club and haven't spotted a single person causing any trouble. It would be useful to climb inside a time machine and go back to exactly when it all happened.

Trouble is that everything is a bit fuzzy. Nobody has said exactly when all of this is supposed to have happened and the only description we've had is of a hoodie which doesn't exist.

I think this is the reason why I'm busy at the moment climbing up a fire escape as quietly as I can.

Keira has managed to get three small cameras which can take pictures automatically and send them to a special machine which she's put inside a cupboard in the gym.

I've no idea how she can get hold of this sort of stuff and suspect she might be a spy. That would explain a lot.

Anyway, we're now on our way to the roof of the building opposite the youth club so that we can install the spy cameras.

Getting onto the roof is the easy bit as we use the fire escape to get there. We've now got to spread out and position the cameras over the whole of the front of the building so that they can see as much of the road opposite as possible.

This is where Wally's special ninja skill comes in handy.

While we set up the easy camera, he's climbed up and over onto a higher roof and is making his way to the far corner.

Luckily it's a cloudy night so there's little chance of our deeds being spotted by any high flying policemen. We're also wearing dark clothes and hoods like proper ninjas.

We move like shadows in the night and soon are floating silently back down the steps of the fire escape when a dog suddenly starts barking.

Did I mention I hate noisy dogs?

Especially noisy dogs who bark at fire escapes.

We quickly backtrack up to the rooftop to look for a different exit.

This could be difficult.

Peter Marney

Trapped

Someone has come out to shout at the dog.

This isn't good.

If their dog keeps barking they might just decide to investigate or worse, call the police. Then we'll really be in trouble.

Actually we're already sort of in trouble but only possibly.

Possibly only turns into actual trouble if we get caught.

The dog shuts up and it's owner goes back to watching the football or whatever's on the telly tonight.

This is both good and bad.

Good that we're not likely to be joined on the roof by any nasty policemen but bad that we can't now use that fire escape.

Why couldn't the dog have been kept inside for another ten minutes? Are we going to be stuck on a roof all night just because some stupid dog decided it needed a poo?

Wally is sent off to explore the far end of the building for other likely exits while we look around the easier bits.

Obviously we can't go climbing down the front of the building onto the main street because we'll probably be seen by someone walking by.

There's less chance of that happening down the side street but the risk is still there.

We can't use the end of the building with the dog either so there's not much left.

Have you seen those films where the roof is nice and flat and the hero gets an easy running leap onto the next building where he finds that flight of stairs leading straight back to ground level?

We could do with that sort of roof here tonight.

Our roof has got lots of skylights and a low wall going around the edge.

We could maybe jump onto the next building but it's only a maybe and there's a long drop and a splatter onto the concrete below. We also haven't a clue whether we can get down off of that building either so decide not to risk the jump just yet.

Wally hasn't found anything and it's starting to rain.

What a nice evening this is turning into.

I'm staring at the various aerials and satellite dishes when I get an idea.

"Keira, are TV men all expert climbers?"

She gives me a look but then realises what I'm thinking.

"No Jamie. I think they'd use the stairs."

If there's an easy way up to the roof then there's an easy way down from the roof as well. We just have to find it.

We also have to break into the building without knowing what's inside and escape without triggering any alarm system if there's one installed. But apart from that we're nearly halfway home.

Wally leads us to a likely doorway then Red takes over. She's got the job of unlocking the door without a key which isn't as difficult as it sounds if you're Red.

Once inside, Keira takes over, leaving me ready to relock the door if we find a good escape route.

She quietly goes down the first flight of stairs with Red behind her.

As Keira carries on to a lower floor, Wally joins Red and I wait until they signal me. We're all totally silent and concentrating on what we need to do.

Red disappears around the corner so I guess that Keira has now gone down to the ground floor. I get a signal from Wally, lock the door to the roof, and move down to the corner as he disappears.

It looks like we've been lucky.

The stairwell has doors off of it at each level but doesn't open directly into any big store space or room. It looks like an internal fire escape which is just what we need.

What we don't need is the big sign on the outside door saying

"This fire exit is alarmed. Penalty for incorrect use £50".

Is that £50 each or do we share, and will we still have to pay it if we get arrested as well?

I don't think my piggy bank can hold £50 and it's well short of that amount at the moment even with the money Gran sent me for my birthday.

We put our heads together so Keira can whisper her plan. I hope it's a good one.

If this is a proper fire exit then, once we're through the door, it should be easy to get away from the building.

If.

Time for action.

Keira hits the door bar and we're all out as the alarm starts ringing. There's no garden so we're straight onto the lane at the back of the building and running for the far corner where Wally and Keira will head off into town, hoods in pocket.

Me and Red also take off our hoods and then slow to a walk to stroll across the road and past the front of the building we've just broken out of.

She's grabbed my arm and is loudly chatting about some mate of hers who fancies her brother but he's still going out with Crystal who is Billy's sister but not the one who's going to have the baby.

There's lots more of this but my ears have closed over in self protection. I hope this is all part of our disguise and that Red doesn't intend to keep it up all the way home.

Then we stop at my bus shelter so that she can give me a cuddle as the police car with the blue flashing light speeds past. That is definitely part of our disguise and a good way of hiding without seeming to hide.

Makes a change from her trying to throw me all over a judo mat though.

Then, as if this was all just normal, she takes my hand and we stroll off down the street and homewards, to meet up with Keira and Wally who hopefully will have found a short cut down the back streets.

I just hope those cameras are worth it.

Window

It's boxing night again but we don't actually get into the gym. This is because Jay is sat in the coffee shop talking to the owner.

Keira wanders over to find out what's happening and I sort of tag along.

It seems the troublemakers struck last night and broke a shop window three doors up. I want to mention that our club wasn't open last night so it can't have been us but now doesn't seem a good time.

The broken shop owner was furious and phoned our owner straight away to complain and called the police and everything.

Keira is excited though because we should be able to see exactly what happened by looking at the spy camera film although she calls them security cameras and forgets to mention how they got put into position.

She borrows a laptop from one of the older boys and then takes it to the magic box she'd put upstairs and plugs it in.

We start with the camera looking at our end of the building and Keira flicks through at high speed until she finds the right time. We all then spend a few minutes looking at an empty street.

The trouble makers must have come from the other direction so Keira switches to the camera covering that end of the building. We should now be able to see exactly who's getting our club into trouble.

Guess what?

Our troublemakers have learned the secret of invisibility.

They must have, because they don't appear on this camera either. The street is as quiet and empty as a very quiet and empty place.

This makes the view from the middle camera even more interesting because it's the one which should have seen the whole breaking window thing.

It's more interesting than we expected but for completely different reasons.

No troublemakers.

Nobody at all really except for the shop owner himself coming out of his front door with a hammer and breaking his own window.

Big Jay is all for going over there right now and sorting the guy out once and for all. I think this means he wants to punch him a few times. He certainly looks angry enough.

Our owner stops him from doing this which probably saves Jay from getting into trouble. He then swears us all to silence about what we've just seen. Something strange is going on here and he needs to think about it first before we take any action.

Why would that shop man want to break his own window and then try to blame our club for it?

Our owner asks Keira to make a copy of the film and then everything gets back to normal and we go upstairs to train.

Big Jay spends five minutes punching the big bag but he doesn't get it to swing as much as Keira did.

Then he starts shouting at all of us to get training and we spend the evening trying to keep out of trouble and out of his way.

I think he's still mad at that other guy.

We don't stay to help tonight so get to leave for our jog home a bit earlier. Either I'm getting slower again or Keira is speeding up. In no time at all we're inside Mr Patel's shop and listening to the week's events.

I sort of drift off a bit and go to look at the magazines.

It's amazing what people will buy magazines about. There's all sorts of different ones and then there's loads of puzzle books as well. I get enough puzzles at school without wanting extra to do at home.

It's about now that I decide to interrupt the conversation.

"Keira, can you buy me a magazine please?"

"No Jamie."

She doesn't even look at me.

"Keira, I really want this magazine."

"Stop it Jamie, I'm talking."

"But it's really, really important Keira."

Now she looks at me.

I think she's getting angry.

"What magazine can be that important to a ten year old boy Jamie?"

Well, they could have one all about dinosaurs but if they do then Mr Patel has already sold out.

I point to the magazine I want.

"Jamie, that's a business magazine. Why on earth would you want that?"

Maybe because it's got a picture on the front of one of the men I saw coming out of that secret meeting when I was at the bus stop.

I think it's a clue to our mystery.

Peter Marney

Memory

I wish I'd kept quiet.

Instead of going home, we're now jogging back to the gym.

Keira made a phone call on her mobile from outside Mr Patel's shop and now we're going back to the club to meet our owner and show him the magazine Keira decided really was important enough to buy for me.

Obviously we can't tell them all about the Red Sock Ninjas, so Keira makes up a story of me waiting at the bus stop by chance when I just happened to see these men coming out of one of the shops.

The owner wants to know exactly what I saw.

"There were seven suspicious looking men who came out of the shop next to the one with the broken window. The first one was this man."

I point to the magazine.

"Are you sure Jamie?"

"Yes. He was wearing a suit just like that one but with a blue stripe. He had a yellow tie and carried a shiny black briefcase just like the one in the picture with that writing on."

Keira explains that the writing are the initials of his name.

I didn't know that grown ups had to have their name on everything just like we do at school.

It's the first question Miss asks if anyone has lost anything.

"Has it got your name on?"

I think if my leg dropped off in class she'd still want to see my name on it before she gave it back to me.

"The next pair were wearing suits as well but not as nice as that one. The tall man had a grey suit and a white shirt with a blue tie. His shoes were grey as well but a bit scuffed. He had short black hair, a bit like a brush, and a big nose."

They all laugh.

What's funny about a big nose?

"The other man was shorter and fatter and was sweating and nearly bald. His suit was dark brown and not big enough. He had those shoes like slippers with tassels on. I think his eyes were blue but it was a bit dark."

I keep going and describe all of the men, with our owner recognising some of them from what I say.

Miss plays a game in class where we have to remember all of the things she has on a tea tray. It's the same game I used to play when I was in cubs and I'm very good at it.

According to Miss, this is because I have an excellent memory although it's just my memory and the only one I've got. I thought it was normal to remember things in detail.

All of this information is very useful according to our owner but I need to keep quiet about it if I want the club to keep going.

I'm not sure I like boxing but I guess the club is a good thing and anyway I don't want to make Big Jay angry with me.

By now it's getting late and our owner gives me and Keira a lift to the corner of my street so we're still able to get home before Mum comes back from wherever she goes with her mates.

The next day Keira meets me and Red on the way home from school. This is unusual so something special must have happened.

She shows me some pictures of men on her phone which our owner has sent her on a guess. He must be good at guessing games because I soon spot the pair who came out right after the man in the magazine.

I think we're getting closer to solving this mystery.

Peter Marney

Following

Do you know how difficult it is to follow someone properly?

Actually it's very easy to follow someone but sooner or later they're going to notice you unless you're really sneaky.

Keira has taught us Red Socks how to do it properly and we work as a team when we want to track someone. I now normally take the role of first follower with Wally some way behind me and Red tracking us from across the road.

 This means that if our suspect stops, like the fat man has just done, I can keep walking past him knowing that Wally will be far enough back not to be noticed but close enough to become the main follower when baldy starts walking again.

 There's no real need to follow him at all because I've already said that he's definitely one of the pair I saw on that night and the same one in the photo on Keira's phone. However it's apparently important enough that I make absolutely certain that this is the correct man and that's why I have to see him again in real life.

 The building he came out of is something to do with the people who work for the government or something. We haven't done any of this stuff in school so I don't know how it all works but Keira

says it's the Planning Department.
I'm not sure what that means and
will ask her later when this is all
over.

For now, I'm replacing Red across
the road so that she can follow
Wally.

If you knew us you'd realise that
something's not right because we're
very busy ignoring each other like
we've never met. We're also just
wandering along and not really
looking at anything in particular.
Ok, maybe we do sort of look in one
direction more than the others but
it's just a coincidence that a fat
bald man happens to be there.

Except that he's not.

He's walked into somewhere where
we can't follow him because, for
some silly reason, kids aren't
allowed in pubs.

Lucky for us, Keira has been
watching all of this and is now
able to stroll into the pub looking
for her imaginary boyfriend while

we keep position and try to look invisible.

This is just as difficult as it sounds.

It's easy to pretend to be walking somewhere which just happened to be in the same direction as your suspect but it's really hard to just stand about on a street without a good reason.

Red's ok, she's stopped to answer her mobile.

Why she gets to have a mobile and I don't is a mystery to me but Mum just says no and it doesn't matter what Red does or any other kid.

Is that fair?

Anyway, I've suddenly developed an interest in books and am looking at the window of a charity shop up the road from the pub. Hopefully Wally has turned around and is now guarding the road from the other end.

We're both waiting for Red to move which will mean that our suspect has come out of the pub and is mobile again. That means he's walking not that he's talking on his phone.

Most people don't know when they're being followed but I think that spies and soldiers and suchlike must get special training so that they can be on their guard. I'm not sure if policemen get this training as well but two of them have just passed my shop window.

At the same time I see Red start walking towards me which means that we're going to be following someone walking the same way as the policemen.

This might become difficult, especially if police do get that special training and they manage to spot us.

I'm using a sneaky trick of watching the reflections in the shop window rather than turning around and staring at people. That's why I can see that Red isn't following the fat man any more but has picked up the other one of the pair from the bus stop. The tall skinny one.

Keira has given up on her boyfriend and is now standing next to me looking in the shop window.

"Is that the other guy?" she whispers.

I nod as I turn and start to follow him, just hoping that he doesn't follow the police.

Following a tall person is a bit easier as they can't get lost in a crowd so I don't have to be too close when I take over from Red.

Just as I'm about to get into position Keira walks by me in a hurry to get to her imaginary meeting.

"Fat man behind us," she says as she whisks by.

Now things are really difficult.

The longer you follow someone the more chance there is that they will notice you. I mean, if a red headed girl happened to be following me for ten minutes or more I think I'd notice and I would definitely be concerned if she was still following me when I'd turned around and was heading in the opposite direction.

I scratch my head as I pass Red which is a secret sign to hurry up and be somewhere else quickly. She wanders into the next shoe shop while I decide to look at the comics in the newsagents three doors up. That leaves Wally who hopefully will now be finding his own way of disappearing.

Time to go home.

Keira comes round later to look after me for the evening and I get to find out what happened after we abandoned our hunt.

Did I mention that Keira is good at guessing games?

When we play Guess the Animal, she nearly always beats me except when I make up things like a flying cow or a purple spotted sea monkey.

She guessed that our tall man might just work at the same place as the other one so she just walked past him and past the policemen and then right into the building and up to the counter.

She gave some story about her brother having a school project to do about our town and asked for some booklets.

Now I can find out what a Planning Department does even though I'm not her brother. I don't even know if she has a brother.

Anyway, while Keira was waiting for the girl to find these booklets, guess who walked into the same building and straight up the stairs as if they worked there?

I told you Keira was good at guessing games.

A mystery sort of solved

It's two weeks later and I keep asking Keira what's going on but she tells me to be patient.

That doesn't mean I have to go to hospital; it's the other type of patient where I don't get to ask questions and have to shut up.

Then one night we go to the gym as usual but end up in the coffee shop again talking to Jay and our owner.

Jay has got some bad news.

"I'm afraid we're being thrown out of the building," he says.

I'm confused.

This sounds terrible but he's got a big grin on his face.

I must be missing something again.

Then our owner explains.

A long time ago, someone had offered to buy his shop but he didn't sell because he wanted our club to keep its home. He's nice like that.

I decide to join the conversation because I think I can understand something at last.

"But if our club starts causing too much trouble, then you might get upset and kick us out so you could sell your shop. Is that right?"

I think I can see what's been happening.

The owner nods.

"But it's better than that Jamie, much better."

He explains that the man with his name on his briefcase is a big businessman who buys up little places and turns them into big shopping areas. This makes him a lot of money.

It seems he wanted to buy all of the shops in our block and turn it into another one of his money making projects.

Our owner isn't sure but he thinks that maybe this man was behind the offer to buy his shop all that time ago.

Anyway, he guessed that the secret meeting I sort of saw meant that everyone else in the block was making a deal to sell their shops to this businessman but our owner was being left out. He reckons they'd decided to create a fuss about kids causing trouble so that he'd then be happy to sell his shop cheaply.

Instead he went and saw this businessman and told him everything I'd seen.

Actually he told a lie.

He said that we'd got it all on film, just like we'd got those shots of the man breaking his own shop window which maybe the police might be interested to have a look at.

I think I'd be convinced about this film if someone told me exactly what everyone was wearing that night and how they looked. After all, how else would you know that sort of information?

Apparently it's not against the law to have a secret meeting but including members of the planning committee before a decision has been reached does suggest something naughty is going on.

From those booklets Keira read to me I now know that the planning people are the ones who decide what can be built where and what's best for the town. I'm not sure that a brand new big shopping centre would be best for all of the small shops we've already got but maybe I don't understand it properly yet.

Our owner suggests to Mr Businessman that for the right price, he might just be willing to sell his shop after all but that right price would have to be maybe double what it's worth. After all, Mr Businessman's going to be making a lot of money so he'll have some to spare.

Enough to spare that perhaps his company would also be willing to support our local community and build a brand new centre for us all to use, including a new youth club.

Now I see why Jay is smiling. Maybe it's the thought of a brand new purpose built gym above this community centre.

Keira explains to me later that some of this is probably illegal and wrong and shouldn't happen. The businessman was secretly paying the planning people so that they would decide to let him build his new project and make a lot of money. That's called bribery and it's supposed to be against the law.

As we couldn't actually prove anything without the pretend film, which we don't have, our owner decided to trick them into paying him a lot of money and also into building us a free community centre.

I still think this is wrong and it's definitely not in any of those nice shiny booklets the planning people produce.

Keira tells me not to worry as, once it's all over and we've got our centre built, someone is going to whisper to the police and suggest they take a look at the deal and especially the bank accounts of two certain planning officers. Then, unless they've been very clever, they might end up going to jail.

That sounds good to me.

Of course, none of this would be possible without the Red Sock Ninja Clan but I don't expect that they'll put up a shiny plate thanking us for the new community centre.

That's the trouble with a secret clan. You've got to stay secret.

Now all we've got to do is go and get our cameras back.

I just hope that noisy dog doesn't need another poo.

The End

Peter Marney

The next book in the series

Why is Jamie being attacked by a small girl who isn't Red and why does he get the feeling that someone is spying on him?

Yet again, the Red Sock Ninja Clan must save the day and this time the cost of failure is too high to imagine.

Peter Marney

About the author

Peter Marney lives by the sea, is just as bad at drawing as Jamie, and falls over if his socks don't have the right day of the week written on them.

On a more serious note, Peter has worked supporting children with reading difficulties and understands some of their problems. He is passionate about the importance of both reading and storytelling to the growing mind.

Peter Marney

The Red Sock Ninja Clan Adventures

Birth of a Ninja

Jamie's about to start another new school and has been told to stay out of trouble. Like that's going to happen!

It's not as if he wants to fight but you've got to help out if a girl's being picked on, right? Even if it does turn out that she's the best fighter in the school and laughs at your odd socks.

Follow Jamie as he makes friends, sorts out a big problem at his school, and discovers that his weird new babysitter knows secret ninja skills.

Peter Marney

Hide and Seek

Find out why Jamie hates dogs and why he's hiding in a school cupboard in the dark. Has it got something to do with Keira's new training games for the Red Sock Ninjas?

The Mystery Intruder

Someone is playing in school after dark and it's not just the Red Sock Ninjas. Maybe Harry knows who it is but he's not talking so Jamie will have to find another way to solve this mystery.

The Mighty Porcupine

What do you do when your enemy is too powerful to fight? Has somebody finally beaten the Red Sock Ninjas?

The Mystery Troublemakers

Someone wants to get Jamie's new youth club into trouble but why?

Maybe the Red Sock Ninjas can find the answer by climbing rooftops or will it just get them into more trouble?

Statty Sticks

Why is Jamie being attacked by a small girl who isn't Red and why does he get the feeling that someone is spying on him?

Has it got anything to do with why his school is in danger and how numbers can lie?

Enemies and Friends

Why has Jamie got a new uncle and why does everyone end up hiding in bushes?

Have the Red Sock Ninjas now found too big a porcupine and will it spell disaster for their future together?

Run Away Success

Where do you run to when everything goes wrong? That's the latest problem for the Red Sock Ninjas and this time Wally isn't around to mastermind the plan.

With the enemy closing in for capture, the friends must split up and disappear. Is this the end of the Clan or the beginning of a whole new experience for Jamie?

Rise and Shine

Why does going to the library get Jamie into a fight and what's that got to do with Keira's plan for getting rid of him?

Helping to put on a show with Miss G was difficult enough without guess who turning up. Yet again the Red Socks must use their skills to save the day and the show.

Rabbits and Spiders

Has Red set up Jamie on a date with Dog Girl? If so, why is he now running around in circles? Maybe it's got something to do with the fact that the enemy have at last found them again.

The Red Sock Ninjas must use all of their skills in this last adventure if they are to escape and live happily ever after.

Printed in Great Britain
by Amazon